The Stray Dog

Retold and
illustrated
by

Marc
Simont

from
a true story
by Reiko Sassa

HARPERCOLLINS PUBLISHERS

The Stray Dog   Copyright © 2001 by Marc Simont
Manufactured in China. All rights reserved.
For information address HarperCollins Children's Books,
a division of HarperCollins Publishers,
10 East 53rd Street, New York, NY 10022.
www.harperchildrens.com

Library of Congress Cataloging-in-Publication Data
Simont, Marc.
    The stray dog / by Marc Simont.
        p.   cm.
    Summary: A family befriends a stray dog, names him Willy, and
decides to keep him.
    ISBN 0-06-028933-3 — ISBN 0-06-028934-1 (lib. bdg.)
    ISBN 0-06-443669-1 (pbk.)
    [1. Dogs—Fiction.]   I. Title.
PZ7.S6058 St   2001   99-45404
[E]—dc21   CIP
                                                                      AC

        11 12 13 SCP 20 19 18 17 16
                              ❖
                    Typography by Al Cetta

To Helen and Jenny

It was a great day for a picnic.

"What's this?" asked the father.

"It's a scruffy little dog," said the mother.

"He looks hungry," said the girl.

"I think he wants to play," said the boy.

The children played with him and taught him
to sit up. They named him Willy. They kept playing
until it was time to go.

"Let's take Willy home," said the children.

"No," said the father.

"He must belong to somebody," explained the mother, "and they would miss him."

On the way home the girl said, "Maybe Willy
doesn't belong to anybody."

monday

tuesday

wednesday

During the week
all the family had
Willy on their minds.

thursday

friday

saturday

"Willy!" they all cried when he appeared.

But Willy didn't stop. Willy was in a big hurry.

"He has no collar. He has no leash," said the dog warden. "This dog is a stray. He doesn't belong to anybody."

The boy took off his belt.
"Here's his collar," he said.
The girl took off her hair
ribbon. "Here's his leash,"
she said. "His name is Willy,
and he belongs to us."

They took Willy home.

And after that . . .

they introduced him to the neighborhood,
where he met some very interesting dogs.

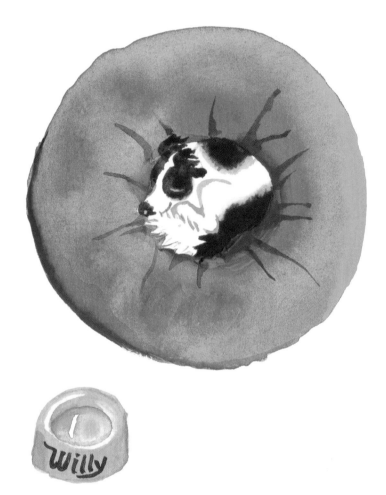

And Willy settled in where he belonged.